CW00327950

from Jandals to Jaffas

THE BEST OF KIWIANA

RANDOM HOUSE
NEW ZEALAND

This edition first published by Random House New Zealand in 2003
Reprinted 2004, 2005
Text © 2003 Stephen Barnett & Richard Wolfe
Design & arrangement © 2003 Random House New Zealand Ltd

ISBN 186941621X
Cover design by Trevor Newman
Inside design by Sharon Grace
Printed through Bookbuilders, Hong Kong

From Jandals to Jaffas is a revised edition of
New Zealand! New Zealand! – In Praise of Kiwiana
First published 1989

Acknowledgement is made to the following for their assistance with this book:
Air New Zealand; Barry Young; Cadbury Confectionery Ltd; Coca-Cola Amatil (NZ) Ltd;
Colin Edgerly; Focus NZ Photo Library Ltd; Foodstuffs (Auckland) Ltd; Geoffrey Short; Goodman
Fielder NZ Ltd; Heinz Wattie's Ltd; Holden NZ Ltd; J.H. Whittaker & Sons Ltd;
Jeff Thomson; K.T. Lawson Group; Keith Money; Masport Ltd; NZ Dairy Foods Ltd;
Paul Thompson; Sandford Industries Ltd; Sanitarium Health Food Company;
Sara Lee Household & Body Care (NZ) Ltd; Tip Top Ice Cream Company Ltd;
Underwood Engineering; Unilever NZ Ltd; Yates NZ Ltd

from Jandals
to Jaffas

Contents

Preface

This book is a lucky-dip into New Zealand's popular culture, that collection of customs, images and objects that have endured over the years to become icons of New Zealand life.

The early settlers, both Maori and European, at first had only what they'd brought with them to this far-flung land. Independence, resilience and the ability to make-do were traits necessary for survival. From the beginning then, New Zealanders were necessarily a robust and inventive bunch, and quickly demonstrated the ability to find new and novel solutions to problems, and to adapt existing ideas to the new environment.

Much of the product of this creativity came to be central to our national identity. This New Zealand 'difference' had its heyday around the middle of last century, before the advent of rapid international transport and telecommunications began the process of evening out the world's cultural differences. In New Zealand this was the era of Plunket babies, British motorcars and quarter-acre sections.

Haere Mai and God Defend
Silver fern, kowhai and sheep
Anzacs, meat pies
Marching girls and mates
Gumboots, Swanndris
All Blacks, baches and beaut
She'll be right.

from Janda

Is to Jaffas

The Land and Identity

New Zealanders are undoubtedly the only nation group whose colloquial identity has been consolidated by a brand of shoe polish. In the early years of European settlement a variety of symbols — predominantly the moa, silver fern, Southern Cross and kiwi — were used to represent the new nation and even as late as 1900 there still wasn't a clear consensus. The silver fern and Southern Cross enjoyed official recognition but it was the kiwi that enjoyed popular appeal, a popularity that was soon to be enhanced by the success of an Australian shoe polish company.

When in 1906 Australian William Ramsay developed a new shoe polish, he named it 'Kiwi' in honour of his wife's country of birth. The kiwi had the additional benefit of being an attractive and conveniently rounded image suited to a polish tin. Further, the name was easily read and pronounced in most languages. In 1914 the advent of the First World War saw a huge demand for polish for the millions of men under arms — leather booted and belted — and for horses' tack. The transference of 'Kiwi' from its association with a boot polish to First World War New Zealand soldiers was then a simple matter. Following the Second World War, 'Kiwi' became synonymous with New Zealanders in general.

Mt Cook

▶ If our National Library is arguably the pinnacle of New Zealand's recorded heritage then it is very appropriate that the library's box number is equivalent to the height, in feet, of the country's highest mountain. As pre-metricators will remember, this was the very easily remembered 12,349. Following metrication, Mt Cook's summit is a somewhat less impressive-sounding 3753 metres. Known to Maori as Aorangi, the Cloud Piercer, the mountain was given its English name by Captain John Stokes of HMS *Acheron* in 1851 in honour of his navigator James Cook. It was first climbed on Christmas Day 1894 by Tom Fyfe, George Graham and Jack Clarke.

Silver Fern

▲ A predominant feature of the New Zealand bush is its ferns; indeed an early colloquial name for the country was 'Fernland'. The tallest of these plants is the tree fern or ponga, and it is the leaf of this species that is one of our best-known national symbols. From the very beginnings of European settlement the fernleaf found its way on to newspaper mastheads and into advertising. Later it came to be incorporated into military and sports badges. It first appeared on the badge of the New Zealand Native rugby team that toured Britain in 1888. It has been used — a silver or white fern on a black background — as the country's sporting emblem ever since.

Greenstone

▲ New Zealand greenstone is a type of nephrite that was very much prized by Maori for making weapons, tools and ornaments. Different varieties of greenstone include the translucent, rich green kahurangi, lighter green kawakawa, and inanga, a more whitish-green stone.

Cabbage Trees

▲ Characteristic of the New Zealand landscape and a major part of our visual heritage is the cabbage tree. Of the four species endemic to New Zealand the best-known is *Cordyline australis*. The cabbage tree is in fact a type of lily, while the 'cabbage' name is thought to derive from British usage of the word in the early 19th century to describe species of palms: early explorers confused the Cordyline with other palms such as nikau.

Kiwi

The kiwi is one of the wonders of this country's fauna, survivor of an offshoot of an evolutionary line that included the now extinct moa. Flightless for thousands of years, the kiwi has only remnant wings hidden under a shaggy, hair-like plumage. Other unusual characteristics include a long bill that has the nostrils at the tip rather than at the base, as in the case of all other birds. In short, then, a unique animal.

Along with the silver fern and moa, the image of the kiwi was used by European colonists to identify themselves with their new land and, while never given any official recognition, the kiwi was, and continues to be, a popular emblem. Undoubtedly the largest and most visible examples of the kiwi in commerce were the big birds advertising Hutton's Kiwi Bacon factories. The kiwis and their accompanying neon signs were designed by Harry Rouse of Claude Neon, and made by that firm. They were installed during the 1960s. Mounted atop buildings in Auckland, Christchurch, Wellington and Palmerston North, the steel and fibreglass kiwis at first rotated, but in later years when the turning gear broke down and proved immensely costly to repair the kiwis were anchored in one position. They were much-loved landmarks on the skylines of their cities, classic advertising sculptures which Auckland photographer Geoffrey Short has described as, 'so long part of their local environment that only strangers would think it odd that somehow kiwis might be a source of bacon'. As Hutton's business evolved the kiwis became redundant and were removed one by one. The last was the Auckland bird which until the late 1980s presided benignly over Kingsland.

Toys for Little Kiwis

The inspired creation of Auckland brothers Hector (Hec) and John Ramsay, the Buzzy Bee has not only been enjoyed as a plaything by little Kiwis, but also has become something of a national symbol. An intriguing concoction of clackety-clack sound, quivering antennae, spinning wings and bold colour, this delightful pull-along toy has been produced in the hundreds of thousands since its first release in the mid 1940s.

Hec Ramsay first ventured into toys with the release of the famous Mary Lou doll

in 1941. It was an immediate hit — generations of New Zealanders were destined to cut their first teeth on its beaded limbs — and soon after other character wooden toys were added, including Richard Rabbit, Oscar Ostrich and Dorable Duck.

The postwar 'baby boom' and import restrictions saw yearly sales of Buzzy Bee in its heyday of the early fifties hit 40,000.

Following a fire at the New Lynn factory in the late 1970s, the Buzzy Bee operation was sold into a number of different hands before its purchase by K. T. Lawson Group, its current owners. While the original cardboard wings — which tended to suffer at the teeth of young children — have been swapped for plastic ones, Buzzy Bee in middle age lives on little altered in appearance.

The famous Fun Ho! trademark was designed in 1939 by E. Mervyn Taylor (1906–1964), a New Zealand artist, typographer and designer whose work did much to create an awareness of good design.

"Fun Ho!"

▶ Fun Ho! toys were to young New Zealanders of the two post-Second World War decades what Matchbox toys were to British children of the same era. Rudimentary in construction but rugged with it, Fun Ho! were our very own sandpit toys. Their origins go back to the mid 1930s when H. J. (Jack) Underwood, a Wellington civil servant, began turning out moulded lead toys in the basement of his home as a hobby. Later he decided to quit his job and go into toymaking full-time, using Fun Ho! as his brand name.

These early models were mostly copies of American and British cast-iron toys belonging to the Underwood children. They met with an enthusiastic reception on the local toy market.

The 1970s saw sweeping changes in import licencing regulations, opening the way to a veritable flood of cheap plastic toys. Sales of Fun Ho! toys plummeted and manufacturing ceased. While the toys were never intended as collectors' items — they were made and marketed as durable, long-lasting knock-about toys — their unrefined appearance added charm, and today they are sought out by a growing number of enthusiasts.

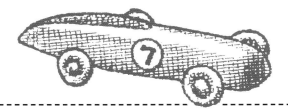

A Sweet Tooth

One thing that hasn't changed much over the years is the range of 'penny-sweets' available to Kiwi children. Such classics as milk bottles, spearmint leaves, Eskimos, jellybabies, pineapple chunks, jelly aeroplanes, raspberries and blackberries are still available today. As for chocolate, Whittaker's famous Peanut Slab is still going strong. J. H. Whittaker and Sons was established in 1896, originally as a distributor of imported chocolate and confectionery, but later turning to manufacturing. Their Peanut Slab has evolved from the 5 lb slabs of chocolate that were common before the advent of automatic moulding machines. These hand-moulded slabs were produced with impressions which enabled the shopkeeper to break off a piece or bar and weigh it before sale.

Jaffa Attack

▲ In the days before television took hold, going to the flicks on a Saturday afternoon — the 1.30 matinée — was a weekend treat. It didn't matter much what was on or that among the shorts might be part six of some adventure serial of which you hadn't seen any of the previous parts. A lot of your schoolmates were there and it was as much a social get-together as cinematic experience. Particularly following the interval when, laden with ice creams and sweets, the now armed and potentially dangerous audience might occasionally let loose — perhaps with ice creams dropped scoop-down from the front circle seats on the heads of hapless stallees beneath. Traditional was the rolling of Jaffas from the back rows down along the inclined wooden floors. And in those less strictly controlled theatres the simmering excitement could sometimes explode with a barrage of Jaffas fired at the screen.

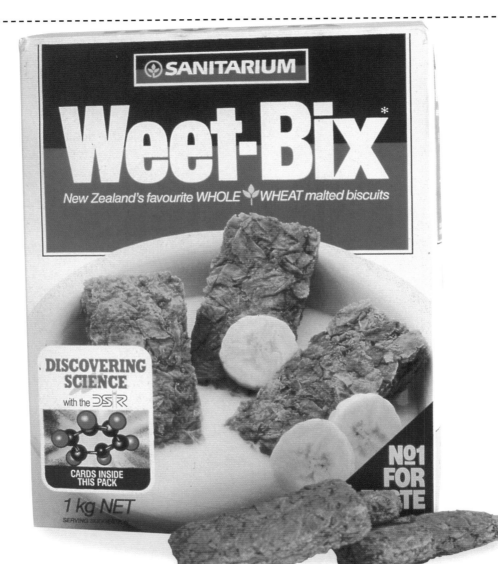

Weet-Bix

Nothing remains the same, not even breakfast. Traditionally, New Zealand's first — and possibly most important — meal of the day was a major event. A bowl of porridge was followed by a laden plate of bacon, eggs and toast, all washed down with a pot of tea. Today, however, the demands on time and a growing awareness of diet have forced a change. The modern breakfast is wholesome, but speedy.

The health-conscious breakfast goes back to the 19th century when sanitariums were places where the infirm retreated to recuperate. The name was adopted by a health food company that had its beginnings in Michigan in the United States and which was to extend its benevolence to New Zealand in 1900. Fully owned and operated by the Seventh-Day Adventist Church, the Sanitarium company practises its maxim that

'Health is Wealth' from three factories. Two of its products are household names above all others, and one — Weet-Bix — is our most popular breakfast cereal of all, hardly surprising given that some people eat it for breakfast, lunch and dinner.

With about 40 percent of the breakfast cereal market, Weet-Bix is consumed by the tonne every day, more than 350,000,000 Weet-Bix each year. For an idea of just how many that is, imagine them laid end to end in a straight line and then driving along that line at 100 kph day and night. It would be 13 days before you passed the last one.

New Zealand is rich in tales of extraordinary Weet-Bix consumption and of feats and habits that constitute a cereal subculture. Eating the biscuits dry, without the assistance of milk, is perhaps the toughest challenge of all.

Chesdale Cheese

A stalwart of school lunches and picnics are the triangular-shaped, smooth-textured, cheese segments and slices made by Chesdale. Deriving from a time when refrigeration was rare, Chesdale processed cheese offered the benefit of keeping well in all seasons. In contrast, ordinary cheese once cut, sweated, became oily, then dried out, cracked, grew mould, began to pong and crumbled. Perhaps even worse. Today Chesdale continues as one of New Zealand's most popular brands and its advertising characters, Ches and Dale, have become something of a Kiwi tradition. Along with 'Broke My Dentures' and 'It Must Be Wattie's' the famous Chesdale advertising jingle is almost part of New Zealand folklore.

Starting life in a block shape, Chesdale was later manufactured in foil-wrapped segments packed in the familiar round tray. Later years saw the advent of individually wrapped Chesdale slices for easy sandwich-making.

'We are the boys from down on the farm,
we really know our cheese.
There's much better value in Chesdale,
it never fails to please.
Chesdale slices thinly, never crumbles, there's
no waste.
And boy, it's got a mighty taste.
Chesdale cheese — it's finest cheddar, made better!'

Quarter-Acre Paradise

For many Kiwis, their home and garden is little short of a microcosm of the colonial estate of their forebears. With no need for actual bushcutting and clearing, today's suburban equivalent is rampant do-it-yourselfism, especially at weekends when the nation's backyards resound with the whine of mowers against a background of power tool whirr, the repetition of hammer blows and engine noise as cars and trailers proceed to the local tip.

A lot of the activity has to do with the country's main domestic building construction of wood and iron. Old villas and bungalows threaten an imminent return to the soil if not for suburban man and woman as Horatius on the bridge, battling against such an eventuality, slowing entropy and restoring order. But the garden and in particular the backyard is becoming less and less the domain it was a generation ago when, for instance, chook-runs were not uncommon and we were as much products of our backyards as of our backgrounds.

With its moist, temperate climate, New Zealand grows grass well, if nothing else. Indeed the country's main earnings are derived from the highly efficient business of grass conversion. In suburbia, of course, with no herds or flocks to keep the grass down, the lawn becomes something of a preoccupation for most householders.

Our most famous lawn-mower had its origins in 1910, when two young New Zealand engineers, Reuben Porter and Harold Mason, went into business together in Auckland. Within a couple of years ▶

their company, Mason and Porter Ltd, had begun to manufacture vacuum pumps and a range of engines. But it was to be in the manufacture of lawn-mowers that 'Masport' became a household name.

The face of lawn-mowing was altered radically one afternoon in 1952 when, in Concorde, NSW, Australia, one Mervyn Victor Richardson connected a small petrol motor to a rotary blade and so gave birth to the Aussie rotary mower. Conventional cylindrical mowers are mostly defeated by the coarse lawn grasses — paspalum for one — which dominate much of Australia and New Zealand suburbia and the greater cutting power of the rotary proved an

Washday

▶ Another feature of every good backyard is of course the clothesline. Early clotheslines were linear affairs, available in flax or heavily galvanised wire. The 1930s housewife was advised to dust the flax line before use, or to check the wire for rust. The 1950s saw the introduction of the compact revolving variety, with the popular all-steel Hills model of 1953 providing 103 feet of line space.

The washing machines that produced the wash that hung on the lines had not convinced everybody at first. Some considered the new machine method less hygienic than the old boiling-rubbing-scrubbing system, but the promise of a washday free from scrubbing on the washboard, the heavy lifting of wet clothes and old-style hand-wringing ensured their increasing popularity. Thus such brand names as Beatty, Washrite, Speed Queen, Bendix and Whiteway entered the language and the laundries of New Zealand.

Laundry soap as we know it began in 1884 when William Hesketh Lever of Lancashire registered the world's first-ever brand name for soap — Sunlight. Demand for the yellow immediate hit. Christening the invention the 'Victa', Mervyn Richardson opened a factory the following year to manufacture his new mower and within five years had sold 100,000 machines.

Surely no name is more familiar to New Zealand gardeners than Yates. The house of Yates goes back to 1879 and the arrival in New Zealand of Arthur Yates. An asthmatic, Yates had come to New Zealand to escape the chill of his hometown of Manchester, where his family were in business as seed merchants. While working on farms during his first few years in this country, Arthur Yates perceived the opportunities in local seed-supply and in 1883 founded Arthur Yates and Company in Auckland, the corporate predecessor of what was to become Yates NZ Ltd. Like another Kiwi brand success-story — Edmonds Sure to Rise baking powder — Yates' business also spawned a book — in this case the *Yates Garden Guide*, now with well over a million copies sold since 1895.

bars proved so great that within four years Lever had built the world's largest soapworks — and a garden village to accommodate the workers. A local soap with a big reputation was Taniwha's Big Golden Bar of Purity, originally manufactured by the Union Oil, Soap and Candle Co. of Auckland.

"I dry my washing in ½ the time!"

ADAMS REVOLVING LINES

here's no need to wait for a stiff ...nd—any fine day is "good drying ...ather" when you use an ADAMS ...olving Line, which spins easily ...e slightest breeze. The ADAMS ...is so compact, too—140ft of ...sufficient for the entire wash) ...minimum of space.

...NTRY CUSTOMERS
...tallation instructions are available, ...y freight to your nearest railway ...station.

...REVOLVING LINES.
...tory: Sylvia Rd., Auckland, N.4.
...79-096.
... send me free literature giving ...particulars and specifications.

NAME.................................
ADDRESS.............................
.................................N.

12 Months'
Guarantee.
Models
from **£7/10/-**

The Corner Store

The death-knell for many small grocery stores began ringing in the 1920s. There was unease about a new type of competition and small grocers and their accumulated goodwill seemed about to be eliminated by the chainstore. This concern prompted the birth of what would later become the Four Square group. However, even with their combined buying power, progress was slow for the new association. The breakthrough came in 1924 when the association became agents for a popular staple, the Te Aroha Dairy Company's Arrow brand butter.

In the same year, while doodling on his calendar, the company secretary came up with a name for the group. His square around the date — the 4th — immediately struck home, and with an Archimedian 'Eureka!', Four Square was born. To announce the new name, a hand-painted glass sign was provided for each store window.

By 1931 the company, now Foodstuffs Ltd, had 112 member stores and a corporate identity was called for. As a result the grocers took a field trip to Howick to check out the colour scheme of a Mr McInnes's store. This meeting presumably approved of the now familiar green, yellow and red livery. But Four Square had to wait another 20 years for its second famous identity, the smiling cartoon grocer with thumbs up and sharpened pencil at the ready. Appropriately, this character was the invention of the managing director, son of the originator of the Four Square symbol.

From then it was all growth: in 1950 'The Dominion's Largest Grocery Chain' boasted 700 stores, and in 1956 it acquired its 1000th member.

'Sure to Rise'

'Sure to Rise', one of New Zealand's most durable, colourful and recognisable trademarks, has its origins in 1879. In that year twenty-year-old Englishman Thomas Edmonds arrived in Lyttelton and set up his own grocer's shop. But business proved sluggish and the enterprising Edmonds sought alternatives. Previous experience with sherbert convinced him to try baking powder. This decided, Edmonds then recognised that the most important feature of his new product would be its name. He even recorded for posterity the very incident that solved the problem. When asked by a disgruntled customer whether her scones would perform any better with this new baking powder, a confident Edmonds replied they were 'sure to rise'. Inspired by his claim he then designed the distinctive rising-sun-with-cakes trademark. Sure to Rise soon became a provincial and national favourite, with sky-rocketing sales.

The *Edmonds Cookbook* reigns supreme among the country's cookbooks: not only is it the country's best-selling book ever, but its total sales almost outnumber New Zealanders themselves. Every home has one, or at least had one. The first (1907) edition, a 50-page booklet, was a thinly disguised promotion for its most vital ingredient. However, it was free, initially, and to encourage good habits was regularly sent to engaged couples. It contained 'economical everyday recipes and cooking hints' in a regularly updated range of mealtime possibilities.

'It must be Wattie's'

During James Wattie's lifetime his products carried his signature as a personal guarantee of quality. That Wattie's became a household name and the company, J. Wattie Canneries, one of the country's biggest, was due to James Wattie's vision of a New Zealand self-sufficient in canned fruit and vegetables.

It was early in the 1930s, when the huge fruit and vegetable surplus of Hawke's Bay would each summer literally rot on the ground for want of a preserving facility, that Wattie saw the opportunity for a local cannery. The venture was a success from the very start. Over the years, canned peaches, spaghetti, tomato sauce, baked beans, fruit salad, asparagus, as well as peas, came to be synonymous with the Wattie name.

One of the company's most memorable promotions was the 'It must be Wattie's' jingle, the first version of which featured ukulele accompaniment. Later reduced to its exclamatory punchline, the complete jingle went:

'If it's rich in flavour and it suits the inner man,
If it saves you money in your household plan,
If it's nourishing and flourishing,
    goodness in the can,
Then it's Wattie's, it must be Wattie's.'

As with most successful ventures, innovation has always been to the fore in the history of Wattie's. It was the first company to introduce quick-frozen foods to the New Zealand market in the late 1940s.

At first, the quick-freeze process froze peas in solid packs. As the competition in quick-frozen foods heated up, James Wattie was keen to be the first to take the next step. He wanted free-flow peas and was determined to have them on the market for Christmas 1958. As it happened, the first blast-freezing tunnel, necessary to produce free-flow products, was late being commissioned. So Wattie had the peas frozen in a plate freezer in trays, then tipped on to a big stainless steel table where staff hit them with hammers and mallets — to produce instant free-flow peas.

Right: *On their way to your table — Wattie's sliced peaches at the filling machine.*

Summertime

The farthest you can ever be from the sea in New Zealand is something like 130 km; in fact it is the residents of Garston, Southland, who must travel furthest for a day at the beach. And also, because the great majority of the country's population lives little more than 10 km from the coast, it's only natural that The Beach should assume such a large role in our lives. Add to that the rich profusion of bathing beaches we enjoy along a coastline of over 6000 km, and it's little wonder that the Christmas holidays see a lemming-like migration from our cities and towns.

Traditionally schooling and commerce have ground to a halt around the middle of December and not started up again until late in January (or the first week in February in the case of schools). From their suburban homes New Zealanders head east or west to settle along the coast like so many migratory birds, making their temporary homes in tents, caravans and baches. For a society already greatly egalitarian, the beach is the final levelling, where labourers and executives, farming folk and townies blend together in a confusion of jandals, shorts and t-shirts, togs and towelling hats.

The popularity of swimming in the sea and the cult of the beach are of comparatively ▶

recent origin, taking hold in the last 100 years or so. At first there were bathing machines and cloaks clasped around the shoulders to keep modestly clad figures from public view. But gradually society's strictures on the matter relaxed . . . up to a point. In 1891 one local borough council declared itself as 'not in favour' of swimming at all by women and girls, and even limited the hours that males could bathe — before 8 am and after 6 pm only. It was a losing battle, however. Not only was the council not able to enforce any swimming curfew, but it also found it impossible to compel male swimmers to use the accepted form of bathing-suit or, in fact, any bathing-suit at all. A greater problem was the abundance of sharks close into shore.

Speedo

◀ The cult of the beach — sun, surf, swimming and sea breeze — is one that is shared on both sides of the Tasman. For many years, summers at the beach were spent clad in a pair of Speedo togs, the label launched in Australia in the mid 1920s as the 'all-Aussie cossie'. Like the first Ford car — available in any colour as long as it was black — the original Speedo cotton-knit swimsuit was available only in navy blue.

Opo

▶ The summer of 1955–56 was marked by the country's encounter with a dolphin. Opo, the dolphin of Opononi came close inshore, playing among the swimmers, leaping out of the water, tossing a beach ball and allowing herself to be handled.

Jandals

▼ The late 1950s saw the birth in New Zealand of a type of casual footwear when Maurice Yock introduced the Jandal. Known elsewhere as flip-flops and thongs, the 'Jandal' — derived from 'Japanese sandal' — first went into production in a Te Papapa garage.

'Jandal' is a registered trademark but like many other brand names has passed into common usage, describing a type of footwear in general. Bata produced their own version, as did Feltex with 'Polynesian thongs'. Much less scrupulous was one manufacturer, believed to be from Taranaki, who supplied garages with a cheaper variant advertised as Jand*e*ls.

The official Jandal spent the first two years of its life being brown and white. Plain colours and candy-stripes followed, but it is blue that has proved the most popular colour.

Tip Top

Today's ice cream giant Tip Top grew from humble beginnings. In the early 1930s the then manager of the Royal Ice Cream factory in Dunedin, Len Malaghan, and one of his customers decided to go it alone. Malaghan, by way of American contacts, had evolved an ice cream recipe of his own and in 1935 he and his new partner, Bert Hayman, left for Wellington and immediately leased premises on Manners Street. Here they opened a new type of shop selling solely ice creams and milk shakes — New Zealand's very first milkbar.

The etymological origins of 'Tip Top' are attributed to a chance overheard remark. In search of a name, and a meal, Malaghan and Hayman were seated in a restaurant when they heard a fellow diner use the term in praise of the service. The expression 'tip top' was then part of the vernacular and widely exploited commercially — hardly surprising in such mountainous country.

Peculiar to New Zealand is its famous hokey-pokey ice cream, a blend of vanilla base with pieces of toffee. Made famous by

Tip Top, it was first sold in this country by the Meadowgold Ice Cream Company of Papatoetoe, Auckland, in the 1940s. The idea of adding toffee to ice cream wasn't new, but what was unique was the distinctive taste imparted by the hokey-pokey toffee.

For many years after Tip Top introduced the flavour in the early 1950s the toffee was formed in large sheets and then broken up with hammers for distribution into the vanilla base. Irregular sized and shaped pieces of toffee caused occasional jamming of the feeding unit and eventually — prompted by the need for reliability required by modern high-volume machines — Tip Top changed to standardised, pelletised hokey-pokey.

Transports of Delight

Through to the end of the 1950s most long-distance travel by Kiwis was either by train or ship. International air travel in the fifties was not yet competitive with ocean liners and, certainly, domestic air travel was eclipsed by New Zealand Railways and Road Services and the interisland ferries.

Railway's steel roads could take you just about anywhere. Thanks to the ambitious public works projects of the late 1870s, the country's main and provincial centres were linked by a network of rail. In the process a lot of dense bush had been cleared and some extremely complex engineering achieved. Massive viaducts had been built to span the numerous ravines, but most remarkable was the Raurimu Spiral which completed the last section of the Main Trunk in the central North Island.

The automobile came to New Zealand in the early 1900s. With the new mobility the car afforded, New Zealanders could now really get around. Shopping excursions and commuting to work aside, Sunday drives, picnics and beach visits were now possible.

The 1920s were barnstorming days of aviation as daring young men and women set all sorts of local records. The first official airmail was delivered from Auckland to Dargaville in ▶

formed around the country and in 1945 three of these were nationalised to become NAC, National Airways Corporation. NAC ruled the sky until 1978 when it merged with Air New Zealand (which itself had replaced TEAL — Tasman Empire Airways Ltd — in 1965).

The first scheduled commercial flight out of New Zealand took place on 30 April 1940 when the TEAL flying-boat *Aotearoa* lifted off the Waitemata Harbour for Australia — a trip that took nine hours. In the mid-fifties DC-6s began to replace the flying-boats, and later in the same decade the DC-6 itself began to give way to jet-propelled Electra. Flying became something that conferred status, and a symbol of this was the TEAL flight bag. The possession of one of those grey plastic zippered bags marked its owner as a member of a special class, and the bags remained in circulation as work bags and for other uses long after the flight was over.

1919, and the following year Cook Strait was conquered in an Avro 540K. The hero of the air was an Australian, Charles Kingsford-Smith, who was first across the Tasman. His three-engined monoplane *Southern Cross* took nearly 14½ hours from Sydney to Christchurch's Wigram airport. Soon an infant commercial aviation industry was providing ordinary citizens with the chance to fly. A number of small airlines had been

Cars, Cars & More Cars

▲ The British cars we loved and drove for a large part of this century were the result in large part of the trade preferences worked out by Great Britain and its Dominions at the 1932 Imperial Conference. American models had dominated sales, but the 1932 agreement made the previously higher priced British cars more than competitive. The works of Detroit gave way to those of Cowley. The roads hummed to cars with wonderful names like Vanguard Spacemaster, Morris Minor, Vauxhall Wyvern and Ford Zephyr.

From the late 1940s this country has shared, with its cousin across the Tasman, a fascination for the first wholly Australian car, the Holden. Roomy, powerful, rugged and well priced, the Holden — and perhaps its FB, EH and EK models especially — came to be part of Kiwi life, as much at home down on the farm as in town.

On the Train

▼ Rail travel has contributed a fair amount of material to our national folk history, and perhaps best known is the refreshment-stop scramble that was once part of travelling on the main trunk lines of both islands. With the abolition of the dining-car in 1917, rail travellers found themselves deposited instead at rail station refreshment rooms and these brief stops — of around 10 minutes or so — became part of the inconvenience, discomfort and, at times, adventure that was rail travel. On the North Island's 'Night Limited', Taihape, Frankton, Taumarunui and Palmerston North were places where you came to, briefly, for sustenance before falling back on your hired pillow for further fitful sleep.

Good Sports

When the obligatory weekend chores of home-improvement and lawn-mowing have been disposed of, New Zealanders turn to their real interests, which usually involve sport. Over the years New Zealand has been promoted as a sportsman's paradise. Nowhere, it has been claimed, is the incentive to play in the open air greater than it is here. Rugby is our national game — a status it will probably never lose. No known meteorological phenomenon can interfere with this most venerated institution: rain, hail or shine, the game goes on.

    If rugby sometimes appears unruly to the uninitiated, it is certainly not a recent development. One of the country's earliest 'games' involved pupils of Christ's College, Christchurch, with a huge number of participants on a paddock. At the centre of it all was an inflated bullock bladder and an unusual set of rules. But New Zealand rugby as we now know it had its origins in Nelson in 1870 in our first club match, between Nelson College and 'The Town'. The same significant year saw our first 'international' when sailors from HMS *Rosario* took on a team from Wellington. However, it was 1882 before the first real international opposition came to these shores, from New South Wales, with the first New Zealand team making the return visit two years later.

    Rugby is a national subculture of immense proportions. At the very bottom of the ladder are the midgets and lowest grades, characterised by their lightness and bare feet.

    When schooldays were over, allegiance was transferred to a local club. Even if this did not prove the stepping stone to provincial representation or All Black-hood it did guarantee camaraderie and after-match functions for life.

Here & Now

JULY 1952   TWO SHILLINGS

Are Marching Girls Decadent?
by A. R. D. Fairburn

MORTGAGE RATES · AMERICAN CULTURE
NOTES ON GARDENING, FILMS, ART, MUSIC
LONDON, PARIS & WASHINGTON LETTERS

Marching

▶ The discipline! The uniforms! The precision! Marching! More than 70 years after its emergence on the national scene — marching, part sport, part performance art — continues to enjoy a special place in our popular culture. Dating from the early years of the Depression marching is a New Zealand phenomenon despite its borrowing from American college drum majorettes. In its heyday in the 1950s, hundreds of teams of Midgets, Juniors and Seniors were going through their drills on sports fields and competing in regional and national competitions, the emphasis on team discipline and appearance.

Eyes right!

Running for Fun

◀ Joggers are undoubtedly members of the country's biggest mass movement, and recognition for putting this country on its feet, literally, must go in the main to one man . . . Arthur Lydiard.

The popularity of jogging in New Zealand

Boundary 6   *Boundary 4*   *Out*

Cricket — a Way of Life

▲ Life is seen by the cricket cognescenti as a metaphor for cricket. As in cricket, you may face the occasional bouncer or risk being caught out in the deep, but each day, like each delivery, provides a chance to play on. At Christ's College, Christchurch, it was not uncommon in years gone by for pairs of schoolboys in chapel congregations to while away the tedium of services by playing a form of the game. The usual rules were followed with each boy representing a team for the duration of a ten-wicket two-innings test. Settled in their pews they would await the scoring as signalled by the umpire, a role played unwittingly by the minister.

grew hot on the heels of the tremendous success had by New Zealand runners, coached by Lydiard, at the Rome Olympics of 1960 and again in Tokyo four years later. Lydiard's training system emphasised strength and stamina and carried Kiwi track athletes to international dominance for the next 20 years.

New Zealand's first jogging club was formed in Auckland in 1962 by Arthur Lydiard and Colin Kay, and within a few short years the deeds of our great middle-distance runners — Peter Snell, Murray Halberg, Barry Magee, Bill Baillie and Ray Puckett — had influenced thousands of less extraordinary Kiwis to don training shoes and take to the parks and footpaths.

L&P

While the label packaging for Lemon & Paeroa has changed often, one element has remained central throughout, the essential lemon. An anatomically correct profile of the fruit once dominated the label, with the drink's name spelt in full. But as the lemon evolved into an oval, the name became simply L&P. This abbreviation acknowledged common usage, and also eliminated a bit of a tongue-twister for non-New Zealanders.

High achievers often have humble origins, and L&P is no exception. It began in a cow paddock in Paeroa where residents discovered a spring that provided a refreshing drink. Some folk, well ahead of their time, were even given to adding a slice of two of lemon to the water for flavour. Before long, the Paeroa Natural Mineral Water Company came into being and began bottling.

At first the beverage was seen more as a therapy than a thirst-quencher, a popular attitude supported by the government balneologist in 1904. Dr Arthur E. Wollman's official analysis described the 'mild alkaline akalybeate water containing a somewhat large proportion of magnesium carbonate' as valuable for medicinal purposes. He saw it as a table water but wasn't sure anyone would go to the expense of bottling it.

Nevertheless, in 1907 Menzies & Co., who already had aerated cordial factories in Te Aroha, Waihi, Hamilton and Thames, took the plunge and purchased the Paeroa company. The company merged to become Grey & Menzies and in 1909 was shipping wooden casks of the water to its Auckland factory. There the water was flavoured and bottled for distribution to an expanding market.

Later, Paeroa's water was analysed and its essential mineral salts identified so that it could be made using water from any source.

LEMON
AND
PAEROA
NATURAL MINERAL
WATER

The Highest Achievement
of the
AERATED WATER BOTTLERS ART

Down on the Farm

For the greater part of the last 150 years farming has played a major role in the nation's economy. And, despite (or perhaps, because of) an increasing urbanisation, many of us continue to feel strongly the pull of the land — an attachment to an idyll of rolling farmland dotted with sheep, a red-roofed farmhouse set about with hydrangeas and daffodils in the spring, hand-fed lambs in the horse paddock, a couple of border collies and a Fordson or Massey Ferguson at the ready.

The stereotypical New Zealander is, to many, a farmer whose pioneer attributes of self-reliance and practical skills still count for something, even half a dozen generations on. The reality is of course a little different, but proof that the concept is a popular one is provided by the huge following that attended the exploits of *Footrot Flats* and its inhabitants. The creation of cartoonist Murray Ball and with what has been described as an appeal to 'cowpat patriotism', *Footrot Flats* was the big New Zealand publishing phenomenon of the recent past.

Art from the Farm

▲ While most corrugated iron ends up on house roofs, shed walls or fences, some of it achieves a more artful end. A lack of success hitching rides during his travels led artist Jeff Thomson to quit putting his thumb out and instead take up walking. The result of his ambulatory travels through rural New Zealand was a keen appreciation of things rustic, in particular rural mailboxes and the ways in which corrugated iron is used on farms. Thomson began producing his own cut and rivetted constructions and it is for these marvellous inventions that he is now best known, ranging from a family of corrugated iron elephants to scores of cows, typewriters and motor-mowers.

51

Sheep breeds at a glance

The six sheep types most numerous on New Zealand farms:

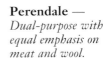

Perendale —
*Dual-purpose with
equal emphasis on
meat and wool.*

Coopworth —
*Dual-purpose breed
with equal emphasis
on meat and wool
production.*

Corriedale —
*Dual-purpose meat
and wool.*

Merino —
*The dominant
breed in New
Zealand during
the 19th century.*

**New Zealand
Halfbred —**
*Dual-purpose
breed with
emphasis on wool.*

**New Zealand
Romney —**
*Dual-purpose with
equal emphasis on
meat and wool.*

▲ New Zealand's 40 million sheep (give or take a few million) are spread out in around 20,000 farms which occupy in total two-fifths of the country's total land area. On all of them the rhythm of the farming year is similar. Lambing gives way to shearing, tupping, crutching and back to lambing. Shearing was traditionally an annual event, sometime in midsummer, but many farmers today shear twice, in July as well as January.

Farm Fashion

▼ First made in 1937 by John McKendrick, a tailor, the Swanndri has become part of New Zealand fashion, the original rugged garment synonymous with bushworking and farming. The original 'swanni', a dark green bushshirt, was quickly adopted by bushmen and farmers for its warmth and proof against showers.

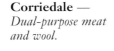

Anchored

▶ 'Anchor' is a trademark that has long been associated with exports of New Zealand dairy products. Internationally known for quality and reliability, its symbol is derived from the anchor tattoo worn by one of the workers on the Waikato farm of Henry Reynolds who gave this name to his butter in 1886. Reynolds later sold his creamery interest to the New Zealand Dairy Association along with the brand, and in 1919 the National Co-operative Dairy Company took it over. Today the Anchor label continues to identify quality exports to a billion-dollar world market.

WIRE

Wired

▲ More than just the wire gauge most commonly used in farm fencing, 'Number 8' has come to be synonymous with Kiwi versatility and innovation. In carving an existence out of the bush — forming farms for grazing and cropping — European settlers depended upon good fences. No. 8 gauge wire came to be strung over New Zealand farms by the thousands of miles. The uses for No. 8 went beyond just fencing, however. Lengths of the galvanised wire were put to a hundred and one uses around the farm and home, including replacement bucket handles and hooks.

Pavlova & Kiwifruit

The origin of New Zealand's national dessert — named for Russian ballerina Anna Pavlova — has long been the subject of debate. The *Australian Encyclopaedia*, for example, credits it to a Perth chef, while the dancer's biographer, Keith Money, is adamant that it was a Wellington hotel chef who, during the New Zealand leg of Pavlova's 1925-26 tour, first made the dish. The story goes that the Wellington chef saw Pavlova dressed in a tutu draped in cabbage roses made from green silk and was immediately inspired to invent a dish that re-created the effect. Hence the meringue case, the shape of the tutu, and the whipped cream, the froth of the tutu's net. Pieces of chinese gooseberry (now kiwifruit) were used to echo the green silk roses.

As for kiwifruit, its international success is inextricably linked with Turners and Growers. Edward Turner, a young English nurseryman, arrived in New Zealand in 1884 and by the mid 1890s had opened a wholesale fruit and vegetable business in Auckland. In 1920 this became Turners and Growers, the shareholders comprising members of Turner's family and the growers themselves. Harvey Turner, one of Edward Turner's nine sons, later ran the company as managing director for over 40 years.

It was at a company meeting in 1959 that the name 'kiwifruit' was coined to replace 'Chinese gooseberry', the name change a response to problems the company was having in trying to launch the fruit on the huge and potentially highly profitable American market. Americans were wary of anything 'Chinese' and there was also confusion over the fruit's classification for duty. US import regulations subjected gooseberries to a high rate of duty, whereas the duty on items not specifically provided for was considerably lower. 'Kiwifruit' fitted the bill. The rest is history.

ANNA PAVLOVA

GRAND OPERA HOUSE

Director : J. C. WILLIAMSON LTD.

Season Commencing SATURDAY, 15th JUNE.

Price 3d.